Stories for Boys

Om
KIDZ

An imprint of Om Books International

Om KIDZ | Om Books International

Reprinted in 2020

Corporate & Editorial Office
A-12, Sector 64, Noida 201 301
Uttar Pradesh, India
Phone: +91 120 477 4100
Email: editorial@ombooks.com
Website: www.ombooksinternational.com

Sales Office
107, Ansari Road, Darya Ganj
New Delhi 110 002, India
Phone: +91 11 4000 9000
Email: sales@ombooks.com
Website: www.ombooks.com

© Om Books International 2013

Retold by: Subhojit Sanyal
Illustrations: Salil Anand, Sijo John, Jithin

ALL RIGHTS RESERVED. No part of this book may be reproduced or
transmitted in any form by any means, electronic or mechanical, including
photocopying and recording, or by any information storage and retrieval
system, except as may be expressly permitted in writing by the publisher.

ISBN : 978-93-81607-42-8

Printed in India

10 9 8 7 6 5 4 3

Contents

The king and the Piglet

Once upon a time, there was a country called Iberia. The king of Iberia was a stubborn old man called Blabsalot. While he ruled over the affairs of the state wisely, Blabsalot had one major flaw — he wanted all the people in his country to do exactly what he wanted, and not what they wanted to do.

The people of Iberia were getting very angry with Blabsalot, because he kept forcing his people to eat only the kind of food that he wanted them to eat, play the games that he thought they should play, and live their lives in the way he thought was right.

Every night, before they went to bed, the people of Iberia would pray for someone to come and make Blabsalot see the error of his ways. But nothing happened, and Blabsalot's silly whims became more and more strict by the day.

One day, in the court of king Blabsalot there arrived a young, handsome man.

"Welcome to Iberia," Blabsalot greeted the young man. "Who are you, young man; and what do you seek in my kingdom?"

The young man replied, "Your Majesty, my name is Smartalot and I come from the distant city of Thinkeria. Your fame has spread far and wide, and I came to Iberia hoping to become a minister at your court!"

The king had been pleased when Smartalot started speaking, but towards the end of Smartalot's speech, Blabsalot had a dark frown on his face.

"It is not for you to decide what you want to become, young Smartalot… It is I who will decide what you can be and not be at court!" replied a grumpy Blabsalot. "I think you are well-suited to be the driver of my horse carriage. You may start work right away!"

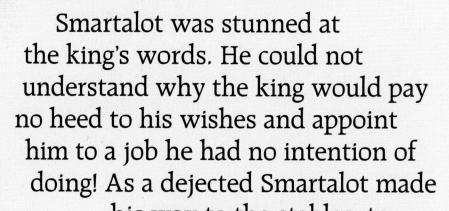

Smartalot was stunned at the king's words. He could not understand why the king would pay no heed to his wishes and appoint him to a job he had no intention of doing! As a dejected Smartalot made his way to the stables, to begin his work as a horse carriage driver, he met the keeper of the royal horses, who was called Neighsalot.

"What happened, my friend? You look like a person who just lost everything. Is everything alright?" asked a concerned Neighsalot.

"I don't understand why the king would not let me become a minister at his court! I know that I am well-suited for the job, but it seemed to me that the king had already decided my future," explained Smartalot.

"Ah, you are new here, therefore you do not understand why the king behaved like that…" Neighsalot went on to explain how the king wanted his subjects to do only what the king believed right.

Smartalot was shocked to hear how the king treated the citizens of his kingdom. Smartalot decided to teach the king a lesson and make him understand that human beings could not be treated like puppets.

The next day, a page arrived to tell Smartalot that the king wished to take a ride through the countryside. Smartalot brought out the carriage, and soon, he was driving the king through the farmlands of Iberia. Blabsalot looked outside the carriage window, at the lush fields passing by. He waved to the farmers who were busy tilling the land, very pleased indeed.

Suddenly, he saw a small piglet playing in the mud in one of the farms. "Stop this carriage at once!" he screamed. Smartalot pulled on the reins of the horses and the carriage came to a screeching halt.

The king jumped out of the carriage and walked over to the mud pool where the piglet was playing. "Whose piglet is this? I demand to know!" he yelled at the farmers who were working there.

The owner of the farm, Mr. Pigsalot came running on hearing the king's scream. "That piglet belongs to me, sire! What has he done?" enquired Mr. Pigsalot.

"How can you let your piglets get dirty by playing around in the mud? All the pigs in my kingdom should be clean and smell very nice!" roared the angry king.

Smartalot realised that this was perhaps the best chance he had to teach the king a lesson. Rushing over to the king, he said, "Sire, I suggest we take this piglet back to the palace and give it a nice bath. Then we can return it to its owner."

The king was pleased on hearing Smartalot's suggestion. He agreed at once, and the piglet was carried back to the palace.

The next day, after the piglet had been properly bathed and cleaned, the king left with Smartalot in the carriage once again, to go back to Mr. Pigsalot's farm.

While on the way, king Blabsalot told Smartalot, "There, now do you see how clean this little piglet is? Doesn't he look so much better? This is why I need to tell my people what they should do! Left to themselves, they will become just as dirty and filthy as this little piglet was yesterday."

As soon as they reached Mr. Pigsalot's farm, the king got off his carriage, with the piglet in his arms, covered with a silk blanket. But as soon as they stepped on the ground, the little piglet started to wriggle out of the king's grasp.

The king was having great difficulty in holding on to the restless piglet and in a little while, the piglet slipped out of the blanket and jumped straight into the mud pool again. He started jumping and playing, and was soon as dirty as when the king had first found him.

"I don't understand," said the king, "the little piglet seems to be so much happier covered in all this filth!"

Smartalot then walked up to king Blabsalot and said, "Because my lord, the piglet wants to play in the mud pool. When he does what he wants, he is very happy."

"What do you mean?" asked king Blabsalot.

"If you let your people do what they want, then your subjects will be very happy. They will honour and respect you even more then," explained Smartalot.

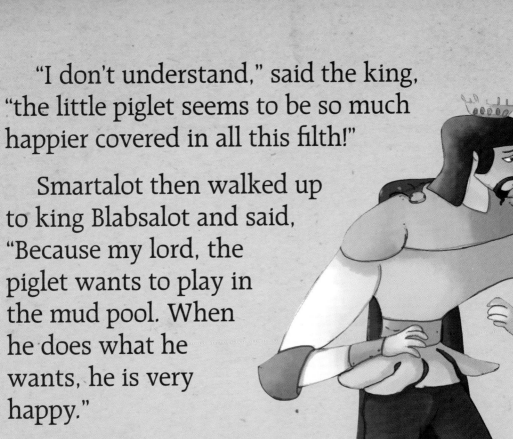

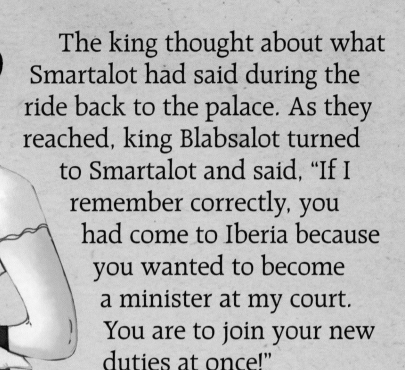

The king thought about what Smartalot had said during the ride back to the palace. As they reached, king Blabsalot turned to Smartalot and said, "If I remember correctly, you had come to Iberia because you wanted to become a minister at my court. You are to join your new duties at once!"

With his wise minister, Smartalot, by his side, king Blabsalot went on to rule wisely for many more years and became the most loved king in the history of Iberia.

Androcles and the Lion

Androcles, a poor slave, was living in extremely terrible conditions. His evil master gave him very little to eat and made him work through the day without rest. If ever Androcles made even the tiniest of mistakes, the master threatened to send him away to Rome, where he would be thrown to the lions!

Androcles kept his head down and worked very hard, trying to escape his master's cruel whip. Then one day, when his master had fallen asleep, Androcles decided to run away. He ran and ran and ran as far as he could; and went into a forest to spend the night. As he lay under a huge tree, shivering because of the cold, he heard the sound of leaves rustling behind him.

As he turned around, Androcles' hair stood on end on seeing a huge lion standing right behind him. Androcles couldn't believe his terrible luck — after all, he had just managed to escape from his evil master, and instead of being able to start life as a free man, he was going to be eaten by this lion.

However, he noticed that the lion was not going to pounce on him. The lion was holding up his paw towards Androcles. Hesitating at first, Androcles finally crept closer to the lion and took his paw in his hands.

The paw was covered in blood and the lion was in great pain because of it. Androcles checked the lion's paw closely and saw that a thorn had lodged itself within the lion's claws. He took the thorn out very carefully and then cleaned the lion's wound. He covered it with leaves, so that the wound would stay dry.

As he finished treating the lion's paw, he felt a rough, wet tongue lick him. The lion then lay down right next to Androcles and went to sleep. He kept the poor slave warm all night. By morning, when Androcles got up, the lion had gone away. Androcles too started on his own way soon after.

Many months went by, when suddenly, Androcles was captured by his evil master. As a punishment for running away, Androcles was sent off to Rome, where he was sent into the arena to fight a lion.

Androcles stood there, in the middle of the arena, sure that he was going to die as a lion walked towards him.

But Androcles and the crowd were extremely surprised, when instead of attacking him, the lion used his rough, wet tongue to lick him all over. It was the same lion whose injured paw he had taken care of!

The emperor, too, could not believe the sight he was seeing. He asked Androcles to explain everything from the beginning. As Androcles finished telling the story about the lion, the emperor told him, "You are a good human being! You are free to go, and you may also take your friend, the lion, with you!"

Androcles and the lion lived together for the rest of their lives. Androcles made sure that the lion was always taken care of, and the lion saw to it that Androcles was never harmed again.

The Fisherman and the Bottle

Fishie-wishie was having a very tough time. All morning, he had been trying his level best to catch some fish, but every time he cast his net in the pond, all he got back was a shoe, a rod and a glass bottle.

He threw the shoe and the rod back into the water, and was about to throw the bottle as well, when suddenly something stopped him. It seemed like the bottle was shining each time he turned it around.

Wondering why a bottle lying under the water would shine like that, Fishie-wishie decided to open it and see what was inside.

But the minute he uncorked the bottle, a huge puff of dust blew out of the mouth of the

bottle. Fishie-wishie tried to stop himself from sneezing, as he saw the puff of dust slowly transform into a whole cloud and settling right on top of his head.

Then slowly, the cloud started taking the shape of a huge beast-like man. Fishie-wishie could not believe what he was seeing. The giant turned to Fishie-wishie and said, "Ah! So it is you who will have to face my wrath!"

Fishie-wishie was taken aback by the angry giant. Mustering enough courage, Fishie-wishie said, "But aren't you the genie who lay trapped inside this bottle? Haven't I set you free by opening the bottle today?"

The genie scratched his chin and replied, "Yes indeed, you have set me free…but since it took you such a lot of time to come by and do it, there is no reward for you but death!"

"What?" exclaimed Fishie-wishie, shocked at the genie's strange logic.

"You see, when I was first trapped inside this bottle," began the sour-tempered genie, "I had promised myself that if anyone would come and set me free, I would grant him three wishes. A hundred years passed and no one came to free me. I then decided that if anyone were to free me, I would give him all the riches in the whole world.

But another hundred years passed by, and I was still living inside the bottle. Finally, I decided that if someone were to free me after three hundred years, I would give him his own kingdom to rule. But even then no one came to free me. I was very angry and I swore that whoever would let me out from the bottle, would face my wrath! Now, after two thousand years trapped inside this bottle, I have finally been set free by you! And now you must die!"

Fishie-wishie, on learning the whole story, was terrified. It seemed that his attempts at doing a good deed would now see him dead. He knew that the only way in which he could outsmart the evil genie was by using his brains. He started thinking desperately for a way out.

Then breaking into a smile, Fishie-wishie said to the genie, "Alright, come on now, that's enough! I can see you are a good magician, but this is just a little difficult to believe!"

The surprised genie had no idea what Fishie-wishie was talking about. "What? Did you just call me a magician?"

"But of course, you are just a magician! Now tell me, where were you hiding all this while? You played a good trick, coming out just as I opened the bottle! Come on, tell me the secret to this magic trick!"

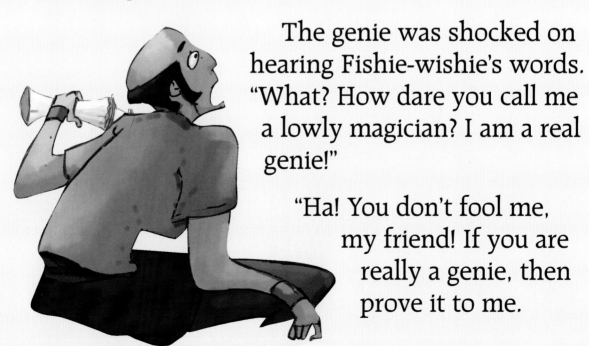

The genie was shocked on hearing Fishie-wishie's words. "What? How dare you call me a lowly magician? I am a real genie!"

"Ha! You don't fool me, my friend! If you are really a genie, then prove it to me.

Get back into the bottle slowly, so that I can see you go in. Only then will I believe that you are a true genie!" said Fishie-wishie cleverly.

"Ah!" began the genie, "that is no problem at all! Just wait and watch!" And so saying, the genie started to turn into a cloud of dust once again. The dust then started moving back into the mouth of the bottle, with the genie saying, "See, here I am going back into the bottle! Now you see, I am a real genie!"

Just as the genie was back in the bottle completely, Fishie-wishie grabbed the cork and pushed it right back into the mouth of the bottle. "You may be a real genie, but you do not have any brains!" declared Fishie-wishie as he threw the bottle back into the water, and saved himself.

Olaf's Treasure

Hans lived in a dairy farm a little outside Amsterdam, in a small village called Cheesetrove. He made the most delicious cheese in the whole of Holland. Every market day, he would load his cart and travel to Amsterdam with the cheese that he had made. People would crowd all around him and buy every last chunk of cheese that he had.

Hans had a younger brother, Olaf, who did not help Hans with making the cheese. Olaf was always busy dreaming. Hans did not mind, and as a matter of fact, he was greatly amused by the dreams that Olaf would narrate to him.

One day, as Hans was working in his dairy farm making cheese, he saw Olaf walking towards him, looking very disturbed.

"What happened, Olaf? Is everything alright? Are you ill?" asked a concerned Hans.

Olaf shook his head very slowly and replied, "It is this dream brother…I have been seeing the same dream for the past three days now!"

Realising that the reason for Olaf's frown was just another dream, Hans felt relieved and couldn't help but break into a little laugh. "Go on, tell me…what have you been dreaming of for the past three days."

"There is a man who keeps telling me to walk to the clock tower in the middle of the market place and walk around it three times. If I were to do that, I am told that I will find a buried treasure and we will be rich for the rest of our lives," declared Olaf.

Hans broke into peals of laughter on hearing this. But in order to humour his brother, he replied, "Sure, I'll take you with me to Amsterdam the next time I go to the market. While I sell my cheese, you can take your walk around the clock-tower."

But Olaf could not wait for the next market day. The next morning, just as the sun started to rise over the horizon, Olaf crept out of the house and started walking towards Amsterdam.

After a few hours, he reached the clock-tower in the marketplace. Without wasting another moment, he started to circle the clock-tower, as he was instructed in his dreams. But alas, even after completing his third circle around the gigantic tower, nothing happened.

Dejected, Olaf sat down on a pile of hay that was lying right below the clock tower. As he wiped his sweat, he heard a voice call out to him, "Hello there, young man! Lost, are you?"

Olaf turned around to find a farmer standing next to him. The kindly man continued, "I saw you circling the clock-tower three times. I thought you were lost. Can I help you in any way?"

Tired, Olaf told the farmer all that he had seen in his dreams. The farmer started laughing as Olaf finished his story and said, "Why, I have seen such a dream myself. It told me to go to this little village called Cheesetrove, and find the dairy farm which made the best cheese in Holland. I was told in the dream that if I were to dig in the barn of this dairy farm, I would find a hidden treasure."

The man continued, "But it was just a dream and I paid no attention to it. Go back home, young man… Your brother must be worried about you!" And so saying, the farmer went on his way.

However, Olaf was stunned when he heard about the man's dream. Though he was very tired after his long journey from Cheesetrove, he hurried back home at once.

Hans was furious when Olaf reached home. But instead of listening to what his brother had

42

to say about his mysterious disappearance in the morning, Olaf grabbed hold of a spade and ran to the barn.

He started digging in the barn, even as a surprised Hans asked him to stop making a mess. There was soil everywhere as Olaf dug deeper and deeper. Suddenly, both brothers heard the sound of Olaf's spade hitting a metal object.

Now Hans too rushed to the spot where Olaf was digging and started to help him. After a little more digging, they found an old trunk lying buried in the ground. As they pulled it out, Hans and Olaf's faces lit up. The trunk was filled with golden coins.

The brothers lived in great comfort after that. Hans continued making the best cheese in Holland and Olaf could never remember the dreams he saw.

Jack and the Beanstalk

Once upon a time, in a little village far away from London, there lived a boy called Jack. Jack lived with his widowed mother and they barely earned enough to have a little food on the table. All through the day, Jack would wonder if there was some way in which he could make some more money.

One day, tired of living in such poor, lowly conditions, Jack's mother asked him to take their family cow, Milky-white to the local market and sell her for some money. Jack was very sad to see Milky-white go, as he was very fond of the cow—but they did not have any other way to earn more money either.

So, Jack finally set off for the market one fair morning, leading Milky-white along by her halter. But even before he could get to the market, one of their neighbours, Mr. Dexterofitis, walked up to him and started looking at Milky-white.

"That's a fine cow you have there Jackie, my boy… Where are you taking her?" asked Mr. Dexterofitis.

"To the market, Mr. Dexterofitis, to sell her. Mother says we need some more money!" replied Jack honestly.

"Ah, good… After all, you will get quite some money for this splendid cow. But you know what? I think I can make you a better offer!" said Mr. Dexterofitis.

"How much will you pay me for the cow, Sir?" Jack asked.

"Five," replied Mr. Dexterofitis.

"I think that will be a little too little, Mr. Dexterofitis. After all, you do agree that Milky-white here is a rather good looking cow!" bargained Jack in all earnest.

"Not five pounds, Jack, I am offering you five magic beans!"

declared the old man. He dug deep into his pockets and took out five very ordinary looking beans and showed them to Jack.

"These beans don't look any different to me than ordinary beans!" Jack replied honestly.

"Ah! But they are not… They are magic beans, laddie! Go home and see for yourself. If nothing happens after you plant these beans in the soil, then you can have your cow back. How's that for a deal?" Mr. Dexterofitis looked eagerly at Jack, hoping that the young boy would agree to his offer.

Both men shook their hands to seal the deal and went off on their own way. Jack kept wriggling the beans in his hands, wondering what magic tricks they would perform. As he reached home, he saw his mother by the washtub, doing the daily washing.

"Ah, I see you have sold Milky-white! Excellent… Quick, tell me how much did you get for that old cow?" his mother asked him even

before he could get inside the house.

Jack dug into his pants' pockets and pulled the magic beans out to show his mother. "Look mother, I got five of these magic beans for Milky-white! Don't you think I got a good bargain?"

Jack's mother was furious with her son. She had sent him to the market to sell the cow and bring back some money, and all he had got back for her were five magic beans. She snatched the beans away, angry at her son, and threw them out of the window. Seeing his mother's temper, Jack ran to his room, to hide.

Lo and behold! Next morning, as Jack opened his eyes, he saw a huge beanstalk right outside his bedroom window. Jack could not understand how a beanstalk could grow right outside his house over one night. He ran outside, and as he stood next to the beanstalk, he realised that he could not even see the end of the tall green stalk as it grew right through the clouds and into the sky.

The magic beans had worked their way into becoming the huge beanstalk!

Not seeing his mother around the house, Jack decided to climb the beanstalk and see if he could find the end of the plant. As he crossed the clouds, Jack found that the beanstalk had come to an end.

He tried keeping his foot on a cloud. It was solid like the floor at home! Very slowly, Jack got off the beanstalk and stood on the clouds. As far as he could see, there were clouds and only clouds — and then he suddenly saw it!

Further away, there stood a huge castle hidden in the clouds. Jack started walking towards the castle, when he noticed a huge woman walking towards him. Seeing Jack, she called out, "You there, you! Who are you, kid? What are you doing here?"

Jack was very hungry, for he had had nothing to eat since the day before. He said, "Madam, I am very hungry! Can you please feed me some breakfast?"

"Breakfast? Have you seen my husband? He is the ogre who lives in the castle. If you don't get out of here right now, he will make you his breakfast!" the giantess warned him.

But Jack was very hungry and made a rather sad face. The giantess was a kind lady, so she asked Jack to come back with her into the castle. Even as Jack started having his breakfast of bread, cheese and milk, the whole room started to shake. Thump, thump, thump was the only sound that Jack could hear.

Jack looked around; he was very scared. The giantess turned to him and said, "Run boy, run! My husband is coming this way and he will be very mad if he sees you! Quick, get inside the oven and stay there!" And so saying, the giantess held the oven door open.

Jack hid inside the oven and saw the Ogre come into the kitchen with two bags of gold. But as soon as he kept his foot inside the kitchen, the Ogre yelled, "Fee-fi-fo-fum, I smell the blood of an Englishman, be he alive or be he dead, I'll have his bones to grind my bread!"

"Oh you and your imagination! Come on, your breakfast is ready," said the giantess. The Ogre took his plate and went out of the kitchen, along with his wife. Jack did not waste another moment. He jumped out of the oven, picked up one bag of gold and ran down the beanstalk as fast as he could.

His mother used the gold very wisely for a long, long time. But when the gold eventually came to an end, Jack knew that he would have to go up through the beanstalk once again and find something else to bring back.

As he reached the edge of the beanstalk in the clouds, he found the kind hearted giantess once again. He went up to her and begged for some food once again. But the giantess first asked him, "Boy, the last time you were here, someone made off with a bag of my husband's gold. Did you have something to do with that?"

"Oh no, Ma'am!" lied Jack.

The giantess seemed pleased with Jack's answer and asked him to follow her to the kitchen, where she gave him something to

eat. Jack was merrily enjoying his meal, when suddenly, he heard the same thump, thump, thump that he had heard the last time.

"Oh no, my husband is coming to eat his lunch! Quick boy, jump into the oven like last time," alerted the giantess and Jack jumped into the large oven obediently.

The minute the Ogre walked into the room, he started sniffing the air around him and said, "Fee-fi-fo-fum, I smell the blood of an Englishman..." But his wife pushed a plate of food before him and said, "Oh stop it now! Where will an Englishman come here from? You and your imagination! Here, eat your lunch quietly!"

The Ogre finished off a huge lunch in a couple of bites and called out to his wife. "Wife, can you get me my hen?"

Jack kept looking through the oven, as the giantess brought a hen from outside and kept it before the Ogre. The huge ugly giant looked at the hen and said, "Lay." And lo and behold, the hen laid a golden egg right before his very eyes!

"I must have that hen… Mother will be very happy with such golden eggs," thought Jack to himself and the minute the

Ogre fell asleep and started snoring, Jack crept out of the oven and ran off with the hen.

Jack and his mother lived very comfortably with the hen laying them a golden egg every time they said "Lay" like the Ogre. But after several days, Jack decided to go back up the beanstalk and see if there were other such fabulous objects for him to steal from the Ogre.

But this time, when Jack reached the Ogre's castle in the clouds, the giantess was not kind to him anymore. "You boy, are a thief! Every time you come up to eat something here, you make off with something or the other. Go away from here right now, before my husband finds you!"

Jack quietly slipped away into the kitchen for he had no intentions of going away.

As he was searching for a place to hide, he once again heard a thump, thump, thump and therefore knew that the Ogre was coming towards the kitchen. Jack hid himself behind a

mop, as the Ogre walked into the kitchen with a harp under his arm.

Placing the harp on the table, the Ogre said, "Sing" and the harp started singing and playing all by itself. It was the most melodious song that Jack had ever heard, and right at that moment, he made up his mind to take the harp back with him.

But suddenly, the Ogre started sniffing the air once again. "Wife, is there a young boy somewhere in the house?" he demanded. The giantess replied from the backyard, "If the boy is still here, he should be hiding in the oven! He is the one who stole your gold and your hen. Catch him and eat him up!"

The Ogre sprung to his feet and ran towards the oven. Little did he know that Jack had by then jumped from his hiding place behind the mop, grabbed the harp and was running towards the beanstalk.

Jack had not even gone out of the kitchen, when the harp itself started screaming, "Help, Master! This boy is kidnapping me!" Within minutes, Jack could almost feel the Ogre's breath on his back, as the terrible giant started to chase him.

Knowing that he had very little time to escape, Jack grabbed on to the beanstalk, the harp secure in his other hand, and slid right back to the ground.

70

As soon as he got back to earth, Jack grabbed an axe that was lying in the yard and cut off the beanstalk.

The Ogre, who had just started climbing down the beanstalk, fell down with the long plant and was never heard of again.

Jack and his mother lived very comfortably for the rest of their lives, thanks to the Ogre's magical possessions.

The Trojan Horse

Long, long ago, when king Agamemnon ruled the great islands of Greece, the neighbouring country of Troy had arrived at Greece to negotiate a peace treaty between the two countries.

However, Prince Paris, the younger brother of Prince Hector of Troy, fell in love with Queen Helen, the wife of Agamemnon's brother, Menelaus. They decided to run away to Troy and spend the rest of their life together.

As soon as Helen's disappearance was discovered by the Greeks, king Agamemnon and Menelaus gathered all their soldiers and set sail across the Aegean Sea, to the land of Troy. They were accompanied by the wise king Odysseus, and the bravest soldier in history, the great Achilles.

The Greeks soon arrived on the beaches of Troy in drones—however, the walls of the city of Troy were high and strong, and even after ten years of fighting, the Greeks could not break into the Trojan capital.

Then one day, king Odysseus heard one Greek soldier tell his friend about how he planned to carry back a small wooden horse from Troy, as a gift for his daughter. Odysseus hit upon a miraculous idea, which could help the Greeks win the war against the Trojans.

Next day, as the Trojan guards took their positions, all they could see was the vast expanse of the sea meeting the sky in the horizon. It seemed that the Greeks had left in their ships! The Trojan War had come to an end!

Naturally, it was a time for great celebrations in Troy. The gates of the city were opened after a long, long time and all the citizens rushed on to the beach, diving into the cool,

inviting waters of the sea. But as king Priam and Prince Paris arrived on the beaches of Troy, they found a huge wooden horse, almost as high as the gates of Troy, standing before them.

Prince Paris, who had lost many of his countrymen and his own brother in the war, did not trust the Greeks, and asked his father to burn down the wooden horse. He suspected the wooden horse to be some kind of a trap. But king Priam argued that the Greeks had surely left the wooden horse as a symbol of peace and therefore, burning the wooden horse would just make them angry.

So, the wooden horse was dragged into the city of Troy and was parked in the plaza, where all the citizens could witness the symbol of Trojan victory after a ten-year long war.

That night, when the entire city had gone to sleep, a trapdoor flew open from the wooden horse and Greek soldiers came pouring out of it. The

wooden horse was full of Greek soldiers, who had remained huddled inside the structure all day long, waiting for the right moment to strike!

Once the Greeks were out of the wooden horse, they first opened the gates of Troy from within, allowing the other Greek soldiers, who had all along been hiding behind a cliff to come inside.

The walls of Troy had been deemed useless by the Greeks!

Once the entire Greek force was inside, it was only a matter of time before the city of Troy was razed to the ground. The Greeks were finally successful in winning the ten-year long Trojan War.

OTHER TITLES IN THIS SERIES

  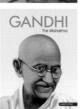   

 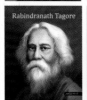   

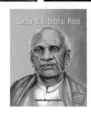  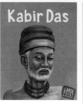